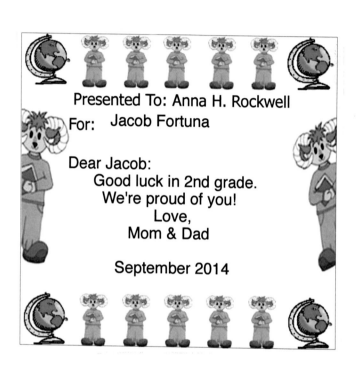

Presented To: Anna H. Rockwell

For: Jacob Fortuna

Dear Jacob:
Good luck in 2nd grade.
We're proud of you!
Love,
Mom & Dad

September 2014

Rockwell Media Center
Whittlesey Drive
Bethel, CT 06801

EROS

God of Love

BY TERI TEMPLE

ILLUSTRATED BY ROBERT SQUIER

Published by The Child's World®
1980 Lookout Drive • Mankato, MN 56003-1705
800-599-READ • www.childsworld.com

Acknowledgments
The Child's World®: Mary Berendes, Publishing Director
The Design Lab: Design and production
Red Line Editorial: Editorial direction

Design elements: Maksym Dragunov/Dreamstime;
Dreamstime

Photographs ©: Shutterstock Images, 5, 29; Jacob Bryant,
10; Malgorzata Kistryn/Shutterstock, 14; Sergii Tsololo/
iStockphoto, 16; Ralf Hettler/iStockphoto, 20; Malgorzata
Kistryn/Shutterstock Images, 22

ISBN 9781614732587
LCCN 2012932431

Printed in the United States of America
Mankato, MN
October 2013
PA02204

CONTENTS

INTRODUCTION

Long ago in ancient Greece and Rome, most people believed that gods and goddesses ruled their world. Storytellers shared the adventures of these gods to help explain all the mysteries in life. The gods were immortal, meaning they lived forever. Their stories were full of love and tragedy, fearsome monsters, brave heroes, and struggles for power. The storytellers wove aspects of Greek customs and beliefs into the tales. Some stories told of the creation of the world and the origins of the gods. Others helped explain natural events such as earthquakes and storms. People believed the tales, which over time became myths.

The ancient Greeks and Romans worshiped the gods by building temples and statues in their honor. They felt the gods would protect and guide them. People passed down the myths through the generations by word of mouth. Later, famous poets such as Homer and Hesiod wrote them down. Today, these myths give us a unique look at what life was like in ancient Greece more than 2,000 years ago.

ANCIENT GREEK SOCIETIES

IN ANCIENT GREECE, CITIES, TOWNS, AND THEIR SURROUNDING FARMLANDS WERE CALLED CITY-STATES. THESE CITY-STATES EACH HAD THEIR OWN GOVERNMENTS. THEY MADE THEIR OWN LAWS. THE INDIVIDUAL CITY-STATES WERE VERY INDEPENDENT. THEY NEVER JOINED TO BECOME ONE WHOLE NATION. THEY DID, HOWEVER, SHARE A COMMON LANGUAGE, RELIGION, AND CULTURE.

MOUNT OLYMPUS
The mountaintop home of the 12 Olympic gods

Aegean Sea

CRETE

ANCIENT GREECE

APHRODITE (af-roh-DY-tee)
Goddess of love and beauty; born of the sea foam; wife of Hephaestus; mother of Eros

ARES (AIR-eez)
God of war; son of Zeus and Hera; possible father of Eros

EREBUS (AIR-i-buhs)
The ancient god of darkness; mate of night; father of day and light

EROS (AIR-ohs)
God of love; son of Aphrodite; one of the original gods at the beginning of creation

GAEA (JEE-uh)
Mother Earth and one of the first elements born to Chaos; mother of the Titans, Cyclopes, and Hecatoncheires

GANYMEDE (GAN-uh-meed)
Cupbearer of the gods; childhood friend of Eros

HELEN (HEL-uhn)
Daughter of Zeus; her kidnapping by Paris caused the Trojan War

JASON (JEY-suhn)
Greek hero who led the Argonauts on a quest to find the Golden Fleece

MEDEA (meh-DEE-uh)
Sorceress wife of Greek hero Jason; helped him obtain the Golden Fleece

NYX (NIKS)
Ancient goddess of night; mate of Erebus; mother of light and day

PARIS (PAR-is)
Trojan prince who caused the Trojan war by kidnapping Helen

PSYCHE (SY-kee)
Goddess of the soul; wife of Eros; originally a human

ARGONAUTS (AHR-guh-nawts)
Crew of 50 heroes who sailed on the Argo with Jason in search of the Golden Fleece

CHAOS (KAY-ahs)
The formless darkness that existed at the beginning of time

COLCHIS, GREECE
A kingdom of Greece where the Argonauts traveled to find the Golden Fleece

OLYMPIAN GODS
Demeter, Hermes, Hephaestus, Aphrodite, Ares, Hera, Zeus, Poseidon, Athena, Apollo, Artemis, and Dionysus

TARTARUS (TAHR-tuh-rus)
The lowest region of the world, part of the underworld; a prison for the defeated Titans and gods; one of the ancient gods

TROJAN WAR
War between the ancient Greeks and Trojans

Ancient Greek poets agreed that Eros was the fairest of all the gods. He was the mischievous god of love. Yet there was a bit of a mystery surrounding Eros. No one could agree when Eros first entered the world or who his parents were. To many ancient Greeks there were two versions of Eros. One was Eros as an ancient god. This elder Eros had no real parents. He had existed since the beginning of time as one of the original gods. The other image of Eros was that of the young winged son of the goddess Aphrodite. No matter which version was believed, Eros played an important role in the ancient myths.

One of the oldest myths tells the tale of the elder god Eros. In the beginning of time there were only darkness and confusion. It was known as Chaos. Out of the swirling emptiness came three beings. They were Gaea, who was Mother Earth; Tartarus, who was the underworld; and Eros, who was the god of love. Eros helped bring order and harmony to Chaos. He played an important role in moving creation forward. It was

Eros's driving force that caused all living beings to mate. Thus Gaea gave birth to the elements. These children of Gaea were the mighty Titans. These giants of the earth would become the parents of the Olympic gods.

Many of the gods on Mount Olympus had famous stories surrounding their births. What made Eros unique was not his birth story though. It was that in many stories he had different parents. Some ancient Greeks believed he was the son of Hermes, the messenger god. Others thought he was the son of Eileithyia, the goddess of childbirth. And some myths named Iris, the goddess of rainbows, and Zephyrus, the god of the West Wind, as Eros's parents.

The Greek playwright Aristophanes gave us his version of the birth of Eros in a play. Aristophanes lived in Athens in the fifth century BC. He claimed Eros was the son of the ancient gods of night and darkness known as Nyx and Erebus. In his play titled *The Birds*, Aristophanes tells how Nyx and Erebus create an egg together. Eros is born when the egg hatches. His birth brings love and light into the world.

COSMIC EGG THEORY

SOME ANCIENT GREEK MYTHS STATE THAT THE WORLD BEGAN WITH A SINGLE EGG. THIS COSMIC EGG WAS LAID BY TIME ITSELF. THE ANCIENT PEOPLE BELIEVED A GOD HATCHED FROM THIS EGG. THE GOD WAS KNOWN BY THE NAMES PHANES, PROTOGONOS, OR EROS. IN THIS TALE, EROS IS A WINGED CREATURE WITH LEGS COVERED WITH SERPENTS. AS THE FIRST RULER OF THE UNIVERSE, EROS GAVE BIRTH TO EVERYTHING THAT CAME AFTERWARD.

The most popular myths about Eros are the ones that include Aphrodite. They do little to clear up the mysteries surrounding Eros though. Was Eros the son of Aphrodite or just her loyal companion? In the early stories, Eros was the companion of Aphrodite. Ancient poets and artists believed he was born along with Aphrodite in the sea. Stories said that in the white foam of the sea there arose a maiden lovely beyond measure. It was Aphrodite, the goddess of love and beauty. At her side were two cherubs. A cherub is an angel in the form of a winged baby. The cherubs were her attendants Eros, the god of love, and Himeros, the god of desire. The image of Aphrodite seated in a shell with two cherubs fluttering around her was popular in ancient art.

The story changes in later versions. Eros becomes the young son of Aphrodite. Ancient Greeks believed his father was the mighty god of war, Ares. Aphrodite was married to Hephaestus, the god of fire. But Hephaestus was so ugly that Aphrodite preferred to spend time with his brother Ares. Ares was much more handsome. Regardless of who his parents were, Eros was fiercely loyal to Aphrodite. He followed her everywhere with his bow and arrows of love and hate.

Eros was charming and beautiful. He was the youngest god on Mount Olympus. However, Eros was known for his naughty and sometimes cruel tricks. His mischief included taking the weapons of the hero Heracles. Eros even took the thunderbolts of Zeus! Eros also liked to play tricks on the monsters of the sea.

Mostly, Eros spent his time prying in the love affairs of gods and humans. His bow and arrows at the ready, Eros enjoyed shooting at his unsuspecting victims. There were two types of arrows to choose from. The gold-tipped ones inspired love. Anyone hit by this type of arrow fell madly in love with the first person they saw. For some unfortunate targets, Eros used the arrows with tips of lead. These arrows caused the receiver to feel coldness or hatred to others. Eros watched nearby and laughed at the trouble he caused. Aphrodite was frustrated by Eros's mischief. Yet she often asked for his help when meddling in others' love lives.

CUPID

THE ANCIENT ROMANS CHANGED THE GOD OF LOVE. EROS EVOLVED INTO THE CHUBBY AND ANGELIC CUPID. HE WAS OFTEN SHOWN WEARING A BLINDFOLD. THE ROMANS ALSO

THOUGHT CUPID SYMBOLIZED LIFE AFTER DEATH. THEY USED HIS IMAGE TO
DECORATE THEIR SARCOPHAGI, WHICH ARE A KIND OF STONE COFFIN. TODAY
WE REMEMBER CUPID MOST OFTEN ON VALENTINE'S DAY, FEBRUARY 14. IT IS THE
HOLIDAY OF LOVE.

Eros had several young friends to help keep him company in the palace. The Erotes were often with Eros. They were youthful winged gods of the various aspects of love. There was Himeros, the god of desire, and Anteros, the god of love returned. The one Eros liked best was Hymenaeus, the god of weddings.

Eros's favorite friend was the beautiful boy Ganymede. Zeus, the king of the gods, was so taken by Ganymede's beauty that he brought him up to Mount Olympus to live among the gods. There in the palace, Ganymede served as the cupbearer to the gods. A cupbearer made sure the cups in the palace were filled with wine. In his spare time, Ganymede often played with Eros. But Eros was not always a nice friend. One of the boys' favorite games was knucklebones. Children in ancient Greece

AQUARIUS CONSTELLATION

AQUARIUS IS A CONSTELLATION OF STARS IN THE SOUTHERN SKY. IT IS THE ELEVENTH SIGN OF THE ZODIAC. ANCIENT GREEKS SAW IN THE STARS THE FORM OF A PERSON CARRYING A PITCHER. THEY BELIEVED IT REPRESENTED THE HANDSOME YOUTH GANYMEDE. THE ANCIENT GREEK MATHEMATICIAN PTOLEMY FIRST IDENTIFIED

played this game with sheep's knuckles. It was similar to the game of jacks. Ganymede and Eros played with golden knucklebones and Eros always seemed to win. Ganymede often left their games unhappy as Eros laughed at his misfortune. But Eros often cheated to win!

When Eros was not causing mischief around the palace, he was causing mischief in love. Eros loved using his arrows on unsuspecting gods and humans. He often interfered in others' love affairs after being insulted by them. And sometimes his mother Aphrodite asked Eros to interfere on her behalf.

One of Eros's victims was the mighty god Apollo. He had insulted Eros's skill as an archer. So Eros decided to teach him a lesson. Eros knew that Apollo liked a wood nymph named Daphne. So he shot Apollo with one of his gold-tipped arrows. When Apollo next saw Daphne, he fell madly in love with her. Eros then shot Daphne with one of his lead-tipped arrows. This caused her to hate all possible suitors. She disliked Apollo so much that she prayed to the gods for help. In turn the gods changed Daphne into a laurel tree. Apollo was not often lucky in love. Eros just laughed. He had gotten his revenge.

Eros then played a role in one of the greatest love stories of all time. The story began with the vanity of three of the goddesses on Mount Olympus. Who was the most beautiful? There was Hera the queen, Athena the warrior, and Aphrodite, the goddess of love. Zeus did not want to make the choice so he asked Paris to decide. Paris was a prince from the city of Troy.

Athena offered Paris wisdom if he chose her. Hera offered him all of Asia. But Aphrodite offered him the chance to marry Helen, the most beautiful woman in the world. It was no contest. Paris chose Aphrodite's offer and set off to claim his bride. But there was a problem: Helen was already married to the king of Sparta.

Eros flew to Sparta and lay in wait. As soon as Paris arrived, Eros shot Helen with a gold-tipped arrow. She fell in love with Paris. Helen then allowed Paris to kidnap her and take her back to Troy. The king of Sparta was furious. He gathered warriors together and set off for Troy. The Trojan War had begun.

THE TROJAN HORSE

THE GREEK ARMY USED A GIANT WOODEN HORSE TO WIN THE WAR AGAINST TROY. THE GREEKS BUILT THE HORSE BIG ENOUGH TO HIDE WARRIORS INSIDE. THEY THEN LEFT IT

The Trojan War lasted for ten long years. In the end, Paris was killed and Helen went back to the king. Eros would never learn, or so it seemed.

OUTSIDE THE WALLS OF TROY. THE REST OF THE GREEK WARRIORS PRETENDED TO SAIL AWAY. THE TROJANS SAW THE HORSE AS A GIFT AND BROUGHT IT INTO THE CITY. THAT NIGHT THE HIDDEN WARRIORS QUIETLY CAME OUT OF THE HORSE AND OPENED THE CITY'S GATES. THE GREEK WARRIORS RUSHED IN AND TOOK THE CITY. THE TROJAN HORSE WON THE WAR FOR THE GREEKS.

Eros meddled in another hero's story. Jason was the son of a king. Jason's uncle had taken over the throne when Jason was just a boy. When Jason grew up, he returned to claim the throne. King Pelias, Jason's uncle, agreed to turn over the kingdom on one condition: Jason had to fetch the Golden Fleece from Colchis. The fleece was the coat of a ram that had once belonged to Zeus. It was a dangerous mission. King Pelias was sure Jason would fail.

Jason agreed and began gathering warriors to go with him on his quest. Fifty warriors and demigods joined him. A demigod is the child of a god and a human. Demigods may be very powerful. Included were Heracles, a Greek hero known for his strength; Orpheus, a human who bravely traveled to the underworld; and Atalanta, a woman who was a skilled hunter. Together they were known as the Argonauts. They set sail for Colchis in a ship called the *Argo*. Jason and the Argonauts endured all sorts of hardships on their journey. They had to fight the monstrous

HARPIES

THE HARPIES WERE HIDEOUS CREATURES. THEY HAD THE BODIES OF BIRDS AND THE FACES OF WOMEN. CRUEL AND FIERCE, THEY WERE USED BY THE GODS TO PUNISH

Harpies. And they sailed through deadly clashing rocks. Finally, the *Argo* arrived in Colchis. Jason and his warriors thought their troubles were nearly over.

Then they met King Aeetes of Colchis. Jason offered the king his services in exchange for the fleece. Secretly King Aeetes just wanted to kill them all. He hated all foreigners. Instead the king told Jason he could have the fleece, but first Jason must plow the king's fields with fire-breathing bulls. Then he had to sow those fields with dragon' teeth, all before dawn.

But the king did not know that Jason had the goddess Hera on his side. Hera knew there was only one person who could help Jason. It was the king's own daughter, Medea. She was a sorceress. Hera asked Aphrodite for help. So Aphrodite sent for her son Eros. She pleaded with him to make Medea fall in love with Jason. She promised to give Eros a beautiful blue and gold enamel ball. Eros loved bright trinkets, so he agreed to help.

Soon Medea was under the love spell of Eros's arrows. She agreed to betray her father. Medea gave Jason a magic salve that would protect him from the fire-breathing bulls. Medea also knew what to do when the planted dragon teeth grew into armed warriors. Finally Medea led Jason to the fleece. She cast a spell on the dragon guarding it. Jason was able to steal the Golden Fleece as the dragon slept. Jason then sailed away with his crew before the dragon woke up.

Eros fell under the spell of his own arrows only once. One day Eros overheard Aphrodite complaining about a human. She was jealous of the beauty of a maiden on Earth. Psyche's beauty attracted admirers from all over. In a jealous fit, Aphrodite demanded that Eros shoot Psyche with one of his arrows. Aphrodite wanted Eros to make Psyche fall in love with the ugliest man on Earth.

Eros set off to fulfill his mother's wishes. But when he saw Psyche, he felt the sting of his own arrow. For the first time, Eros fell in love. He began visiting Psyche, but only at night. Eros hid himself in the dark and asked Psyche not to light her lamp. But Psyche was curious to see this stranger. One night Psyche lit her lamp as Eros slept. She realized it was the god of love at her side. When a drop of oil fell on Eros's brow, he awoke. Angry that Psyche had betrayed his trust, Eros fled to Mount Olympus.

Psyche was upset yet determined. She roamed the earth in search of her one true love. Eventually she prayed to the goddess Aphrodite for help. At first Aphrodite placed a series of tasks before Psyche. Eventually Aphrodite gave in. Zeus gave Eros permission to marry Psyche. Together they lived on Mount Olympus.

Eros was worshipped along with his mother. As the gods of love they would always have followers. The ancient town of Thespiae, Greece, was a special place for Eros. Eros's followers worshiped him there with only a crude stone as a symbol of the god. Later in the fourth century BC, a sculptor named Praxiteles created one of the most famous statues of the ancient world near the foot of Mount Helicon. Praxiteles made this Eros statue out of bronze. It was destroyed in a great fire in 80 AD. The Thespians also celebrated Eros with a festival. The Erotidia was held every five years to honor Eros.

Eros could tame the hearts of men and beasts. Yet the hero Perseus once warned Eros to help those in love to succeed. Perseus knew that humans would then honor Eros. If Eros did not help, he would lose the gratitude of all those he touched. We may never know the answers to the questions surrounding Eros. Still, his myths and legends will endure. Eros is sure to inspire artists, writers, and dreamers far into the future.

WORSHIP IN ANCIENT GREECE

ANCIENT GREEKS WORSHIPED MAINLY IN TEMPLES. THESE TEMPLES CONTAINED A STATUE DEDICATED TO A SPECIFIC GOD. EACH CITY-STATE HAD ITS OWN FAVORITE GOD. THE ANCIENT PEOPLE HELD FESTIVALS TO HONOR THE GODS. THEY WOULD CREATE DANCES, PLAYS, AND POETRY TO SING THE PRAISES OF THEIR GOD. SACRIFICE ALSO PLAYED AN IMPORTANT ROLE IN WORSHIP. IT WAS IMPORTANT TO KEEP THE GODS HAPPY.

PRINCIPAL GODS OF GREEK MYTHOLOGY – A FAMILY TREE

EROS

ARES   HEBE   HEPHAESTUS   ATHENA   PERSEPHONE   APOLLO   ARTEMIS   HERMES   APHRODITE

ZEUS   MAIA   ZEUS   DIONE

POSEIDON   HADES   HESTIA   HERA   ZEUS   DEMETER   ATLAS   PROMETHEUS   EPIMETHEUS

IAPETUS

CRONUS   RHEA   LETO   ZEUS   COEUS   PHOEBE   OCEANUS   TETHYS

GAEA
(Earth)
URANUS
(Heaven)

THE ROMAN GODS

As the Roman Empire expanded by conquering new lands the Romans often took on aspects of the customs and beliefs of the people they conquered. From the ancient Greeks they took their arts and sciences. They also adopted many of their gods and the myths that went with them into their religious beliefs. While the names were changed, the stories and legends found a new home.

ZEUS: *Jupiter*
King of the Gods, God of Sky and Storms
Symbols: *Eagle and Thunderbolt*

HERA: *Juno*
Queen of the Gods, Goddess of Marriage
Symbols: *Peacock, Cow, and Crow*

POSEIDON: *Neptune*
God of the Sea and Earthquakes
Symbols: *Trident, Horse, and Dolphin*

HADES: *Pluto*
God of the Underworld
Symbols: *Helmet, Metals, and Jewels*

ATHENA: *Minerva*
Goddess of Wisdom, War, and Crafts
Symbols: *Owl, Shield, and Olive Branch*

ARES: *Mars*
God of War
Symbols: *Vulture and Dog*

ARTEMIS: *Diana*
Goddess of Hunting and Protector of Animals
Symbols: *Stag and Moon*

APOLLO: *Apollo*
God of the Sun, Healing, Music, and Poetry
Symbols: *Laurel, Lyre, Bow, and Raven*

HEPHAESTUS: *Vulcan*
God of Fire, Metalwork, and Building
Symbols: *Fire, Hammer, and Donkey*

APHRODITE: *Venus*
Goddess of Love and Beauty
Symbols: *Dove, Sparrow, Swan, and Myrtle*

EROS: *Cupid*
God of Love
Symbols: *Quiver and Arrows*

HERMES: *Mercury*
God of Travels and Trade
Symbols: *Staff, Winged Sandals, and Helmet*

FURTHER INFORMATION

BOOKS

Green, Jen. *Ancient Greek Myths*. New York: Gareth Stevens, 2010.

Napoli, Donna Jo. *Treasury of Greek Mythology: Classic Stories of Gods, Goddesses, Heroes & Monsters*. Washington, DC: National Geographic Society, 2011.

Turnbull, Ann. *Greek Myths*. Somerville, MA: Candlewick Press, 2011.

WEB SITES

Visit our Web site for links about Eros: **childsworld.com/links**

Note to Parents, Teachers, and Librarians: We routinely verify our Web links to make sure they are safe and active sites. So encourage your readers to check them out!

INDEX

Rockwell Media Center
Whittlesey Drive
Bethel, CT 06801